Majestic

~Midnight Crest Series Book One~

KAY MAREE

Contents

Blurb

A man trapped in darkness.
A woman unable to escape the heartbreak of her past.
And, the magical powers of a Majestic waterfall which
brings these two together.

Cover – Susan Horsnell
Editing – Susan Horsnell & Word Writer Pro

Social Links

Facebook:
https://www.facebook.com/kay.maree.334
Twitter:
https://twitter.com/MisKay85
Goodreads:
https://www.goodreads.com/book/show/34528910-
angel-mine?ac=1&from_search=true
Goodreads Author Page:
https://www.goodreads.com/user/show/65394903-kay-
maree

I live in Newcastle, on the New South Wales coast of Australia with my husband and three beautiful children.

Between being a taxi for my children, and working full-time, I somehow find the time to write. It's something I love with a passion and with the encouragement of my very supportive husband, I have accomplished one of my dreams – releasing my first novel.

I hope you fall in love with my characters as much as I have.

I love reading and getting lost in a good book when I manage to snatch five minutes to myself.

Kay Maree

Dedication

To all the women in my group who push me every day to
try harder.
You ladies are amazing and without you in my corner, I
wouldn't be where I am today.
Thank you.

To my beautiful friend and editor, Susan, thank you for
always been patient with me and dealing with my crazy on
a day to day basis.

Chapter One

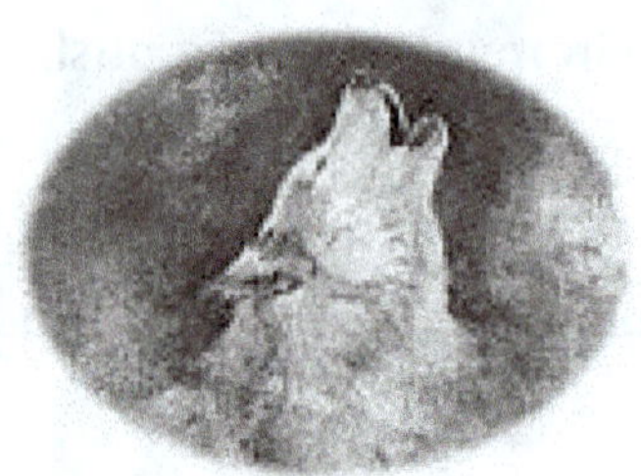

Emerson

I smile for the first time today at the sight of the beautiful waterfall revealed when I push through the clearing. Moving quickly to the water's edge, I drop my shoulder bag to the ground beside me, it hits with a dull thud. Dropping to my knees, beside me, I run my fingertips through the shining water and hope it can help me today. My heart has felt heavy all day, I need to feel centered again and this majestic waterfall seems to do just that.

I miss them more than ever and feel so alone. It always astounds me, how one simple touch, feeling the coolness of the water against my fingertips, can send tingles racing through me. It's as if I'm alive for the first time in a long time.

Resting back on my heels, I close my eyes and feel the hot tears spill down my cheeks. I release the breath I hadn't realized I was holding. Emotions run rampant through me. I have cried so many tears into this waterfall, it wouldn't surprise me if the water was only my tears.

I cry for the family I've lost and I weep, because no matter what I do, I believe it isn't good enough. The bright sun shines down through the trees and the water appears to be speckled with diamonds. I tilt my head back and it warms my face. I wonder, if I drink enough of this magical water will it dull the ache inside me, fill my heart and make me shine. Rid me of the false bravado I use every day, hoping everybody is fooled. I hear the whispers around town – *she's too quiet* and *not social enough*, but I can't seem to break through my own walls to allow someone in.

Am I afraid of getting hurt again?

Maybe.

~

Looking back at the water, I watch as it crashes down over centuries old rocks to rest in the crystal-clear pool below. The sound washes over me, warms me, gives me strength. It makes it simple to believe I can change and push forward, but it's a never-ending battle each and every day.

I think back to the person I once was - a fighter. I pushed through the hard times knowing there was always something waiting for me on the other side which would make it worth the fight. But, when my parents were taken from me, I lost myself. I really wish I could get *me* back. I'm not this mousy little girl everyone thinks I am, but before I can show my true self to the world, I need to find myself. Prove that I'm still the same old me, but stronger and with a few more scars on my heart.

~

I work in the local library in town and apart from this majestic waterfall, it's the only other place I feel centered. It enfolds me in a world where I get lost in the stacks and the smell of pages promising endless love stories. At one time, I had it all. A loving family, a man I thought adored me, but although I thought him a prince, he turned into a toad.

Twenty-six years old, that was my age when everything came crashing down and my life changed. When I lost my parents, I couldn't stand being in my old town anymore. I knew everyone blamed me for their deaths so, I moved myself, lock stock and barrel to Millaa Millaa Falls. I had heard a lot of stories about this place, but it was the waterfall which really drew me. The diamond water seems to heal my soul. Eight months have passed since I moved here, I needed to branch out and move forward, but I think the opposite happened. I retreated deeper into my bubble and I pray one day I can break free.

At night when I close my eyes is the most difficult, knowing when I wake, I'll still be here and even lonelier than the day before. When I sleep, a pair of liquid lead colored eyes with specks of emeralds invade my dreams. They calm me and I feel more loved than I have in a long time, but I wonder if he'll catch me when I fall. There's a sadness in his eyes, but also a hunger which sends shivers racing down my spine causing goosebumps to appear. He reaches for me, but only the tips of his fingers brush me before I wake in a cold sweat.

Every night, when I return home after visiting the waterfall, this dream invades my sleep. It started about a month after I moved here. At first, I brushed it off, not wanting to think about a man with eyes more captivating and enchanting than any I'd seen before. But, as time passes, it gets harder and harder to ignore it. I'm not sure what the dream means and I don't know if I ever want to be vulnerable again, allow someone in.

The toad cracked me, the death of my parents shattered me. Being here is healing me and for some strange unknown reason, when I gaze into the eyes of this unknown man, I want him to piece me back together. I don't know if I'm strong enough to let anyone know my story. I came here clean and untouched. Emerson, the too quiet librarian with oversized glasses and sad eyes.

Chapter Two

Raff

I relax back in my chair, bring the cup to my lips and sip at the hot brew. This is the best part of my day. I gaze out my office window, mesmerized by the beautiful dark-haired goddess below. She is on her knees by the waterfall's edge, caressing the water with the tips of her fingers, causing it to ripple around them. I hear her soft cries rising on the breeze toward me and the gasps as she sucks in air between sobs. Her cries and sobs have permeated me to the bone for longer than I can remember. Again, I wish I could take her pain away. I want to rush down to her, help take her pains away. My chest tightens as I fight the urge and I squeeze my eyes shut. I'm not the man she needs.

My life is in this home I have built, secluded high up in the trees, away from humanity. Once, I ventured out only at night, when the town beneath me slept and there was no risk of discovery. But, things have changed. I have been leaving the safety of my home during the sunlit hours, wanting to be nearer to the woman whose heart is breaking. The woman whose anguish touches my heart. I don't dare get near enough to touch her, or let her know I'm close by, but enough to make sure she returns safely home. I've caused so much hurt and I couldn't bear to inflict my past on someone else, especially this woman. Her hurt and upset has my heart beating faster, my body twitching, on full alert. To calm myself, because I know she's safe, I drag in a deep breath and blow it out slowly. I focus on her glossy hair, lifted by the light breeze and know I have made the right decision to stay away from her. So, fighting the urge to rush to her side, I sit and watch from afar. I imagine a life where I had the ability to make a woman happy. Not just any woman, this woman.

When I close my eyes at night, she comes to me, fills my dreams. Her skin fair, like the clouds above. Eyes, the palest of blues, which glow and sparkle like the clearest water and a smile that rivals any sunrise. I reach out to hold her, if only for a moment. But, my fingertips only graze skin so soft it reminds me of feathers. Then, she's gone. Even in my dreams, I'm prevented from touching her. Maybe they aren't dreams, but nightmares, reminding me that nothing good can be touched by the likes of me. When I wake, I recall her smile and the way it lights up her face. Her adoring eyes, convinced I am her knight in shining armor, here to rescue her from the darkness. But, I can't be that man for I am the darkness she needs rescuing from. I hurt people, not by choice, none of this is my choice. I was brought into the world this way. Being here, high in the trees, I can control the beast living inside me. On the ground, being close to the woman, I don't think I could.

~

The mere hint of her sweet scent drifting on the air has my wolf clawing to the surface, wanting to break free. It takes every ounce of my strength to hold him back. For eight long, excruciating months he has known as well as I do, this woman is our true mate. When I moved here over a year ago, I hoped the calming waters with majestic

11

powers would soothe, possibly heal me. Instead, I'm tortured, knowing the one thing I want, I can't have.

I lean back in the chair and drag my fingers through my long brown hair. I'm frustrated with myself. Why the hell haven't I moved away from this place? To save us both from heartbreak because I don't know how much longer I can hold him back from her. Every day feels like I'm fighting a losing battle and the wolf pushes forward a little more. I admit the truth, we haven't left because of the need to protect her and keep her safe. But, what happens when the day comes and she brings a man into our sanctuary? I know I will lose what control I have and the wolf will surge forward and take what is rightfully his.

Chapter Three

Emerson

I sense a strong force pulling deep down in my core whenever I come here. The soothing, yet eerie falls hold a great deal more than my tears and secrets of a past life I've destroyed. It's more than just me and the peaceful hum of the water falling. It's carnal, hot and hellishly undefined. I love it. Sweat pools at the base of my spine as goose bumps caused by *what ifs* and dire need prickle my skin.

Something - a flicker of bright silver light catches my eye and I lift my head. My eyes scan the vast and beautiful forest surrounding this heaven, but I can't seem to catch it again. Disbursed on the light breeze which lifts my long, inky black locks on a sensuous dance around me. The sun sinks slowly behind the waterfall and the sky is lit by the beautiful warmth of pinkish reds and yellowish oranges. The diamond water comes alive, shimmers and glows. I fold my arms around myself to ward off the crisp chill descending with the twilight of dusk.

The time has come for me to leave, reluctantly I stand, stretch my legs and lean forward to retrieve my backpack. My head snaps around when I'm alerted by a sound, my senses on full alert, senses heightened by this location. Peering into the disappearing light, I see nothing so I shrug it off and head toward the clearing which leads me away from my paradise.

~

I take my time crossing the clearing to where my Ford Laser is parked. Not a luxury car by any means, but it serves me well and runs on the smell of an oily rag. My fingers dance along her chipped and fading silver paint as I make my way to the driver's side door. My hand stops on the handle as I hear a rev? It sounds like the throaty rev of a high-powered engine from somewhere down the dirt road. I peer into the distance as bright lights are flicked on, blinding me to all else. Screaming tires, lights bobbing on the uneven road, come at me fast. I can't move, my legs are frozen in place. Why? My heart thuds in my ears, breath catches in my lungs. I feel like I'm being starved of air. I attempt to lift my arms, shield my eyes, but they feel heavy, glued to my sides. The lights are moving faster, closer. The scream of the engine louder as it approaches. Then, a deep throaty growl echoes off the trees. Before I can figure out where the sound has come from, I'm flying through the air, skidding along the dirt track. My head smacks into the earth, the force bouncing it back up before it crashes down again. When I finally come to a stop, a cloud of dust surrounds me.

"Holy shit," I groan. Tentatively raising fingers to the base of my skull, I feel a wet patch. Lowering my hand to where I can see as the final rays of sunset dance in the sky, I note the crimson red of blood. Wiggling my fingers in the dim light, I watch as the blood seems to glitter. *What the fuck, why the hell is my blood glittering?* A slight sound draws my eyes to another pair - liquid grey sprinkled with emerald chips. Piercing in a way which seems to see straight through me. I shake my head to clear the woozy feeling, maybe that's why my blood seems to shimmer, I'm hallucinating. I look back, they're still there. Watching. Focused. The eyes of my dreams. As I reach out, my eyelids become heavy, darkness like an inky black cloak wraps around me and I crumple to the ground.

Chapter Four

Raff

I'm drawn to her; my eyes locked on the rise and fall of her chest, the swell of her breasts. Noting every dip and curve of her body, my teeth ache, wanting a taste. She looks tiny laying in the large, wooden four poster bed.

The image of holding her in my arms earlier is burnt into my memory, never to leave. The way her body rested against mine, molded perfectly into me. She is the final piece of my puzzle, coming home to where she belongs. The one I have been waiting for my whole life. The one who will quell the anger and mend the pain.

Standing stone still, I watch her. I fight with all I am to calm my rapid breathing and the carnal growls bubbling at the back of my throat. She should never have been in my arms, or in my fucken bed now. What the hell have I done, what have I allowed to happen? I can no longer fight this need, I can't let her go. She belongs here, her body relaxed into the plush duvet of my bed, her inky black hair fanned out over the crisp white linen of the pillows.

She belongs with me. The faint smell of Jasmine encompasses the room, surrounds me, captivates me, draws me in and overwhelms my senses. It takes my carnal soul on a rollercoaster ride of emotions which I have tried to bury for the past few moons.

~

She needs to rest and I need to figure out what needs to be done. Why in the hell would someone, here of all places, be wanting to hurt her. Before turning toward the door, I steal one last glance to make sure she is here, real and safe. I close the door with a soft click after leaving the room, not wanting to wake my sleeping beauty. She took one hell of a hit to her head, I hadn't meant to be so forceful, but there was some kind of force surrounding her. Something that grounded her and kept her in place, in danger. I had to use more strength to move her, to take her out of the path of the vehicle speeding toward her. The cut to the back of her head is minor and will heal fine, but she'll need to be watched. She remained unconscious as I carried her here, whimpering slightly only when I laid her down on the bed.

She'll probably have one hell of a headache when she wakes, but better that than being dead. *Shit, she's going to wake up here in my bed*. The thought has a pain gripping my chest, slamming the air from my lungs I need to calm down and think before I do something I'll regret. Moving to the window in my living room, I open it to allow air into this hot as fuck room which is overflowed with her scent. I reach down and take my shirt off, bring it up to my nose and it's like breathing in pure, fucking sunshine. My senses are going fucking nuts and it takes everything in me to not climb out of my skin.

After tossing the shirt to the floor, I look through the window again. Something catches my eye, a bright flicker of light. What the hell? My senses are on overdrive right now, this is making it worse. It's the same eerie feeling I had right before car lights flashed on and a car sped straight toward my woman. I serach the darkness for what could be out there, a noise floats in on the wind laced with a warning. Something's not right and whatever is out there is not going to be good.

~

Turning and pacing, I replay the events of the night on a loop in my mind. The car, the driver. Everything happened so fast. I didn't get a good look at who was behind the wheel, but the sense of knowing was strong, it still is. I can't shake the feeling of knowing the person, but here, now, why? I couldn't give it much thought at the time, I was more worried about getting to my woman. *Ah fuck, now I'm calling her my women like I have ownership over her. Oh, fuck yes, I do. She just doesn't know it yet.*

Fuck, I need to sort my shit out and focus. Cracking my neck, I move to my desk which overlooks the waterfall. The sound of the water crashing down usually soothes me, but tonight it's not doing shit. I'm too much on edge. Placing my hands down flat on the rough wood surface, I push down with such force, my knuckles turn white. My muscles jump and flex, the tightening in my chest has me taking deep breaths. I close my eyes, feeling the ripples under my skin, my eye color will have changed, he's pushing to break free. I need to figure this shit out and fast.

I drag my focus back to the task at hand and away from my wolf wanting to break free I use what little control I have left to push him back down. After a moment, I feel myself relax and my breathing steadies.

I know I need to look into what might be happening, but I don't want to leave her side. Correction, I can't leave her side and I won't.

She is *Mine*.

~

My chest tightens at the thought of leaving my mate alone and I shake my head. "Fuck, what the hell have I done?" I growl low to the empty room. Gripping my head in both hands and blowing out a deep breath, I sink into my chair. "Fuck!" Standing again, I gaze through the large picture window, staring out at the dark forest and listening to the waterfall crashing over the rocks. When I hear a faint sound, my eyes widen, peering into the distance, searching the darkness. I can't pinpoint where it is or what it is. Just like that, it fades away as quick as it came. *What the fuck is happening?* I had the same heightened sense when the car tried to run my mate down. I continue looking, searching the vast forest, but nothing. When I start to turn away, I catch the glint of two small red lights, I assume they are lights. They seem to flash fast and out of my view. It's strange for me to not get a good look, or feel, as my senses and abilities are stronger, faster and more heightened than most creatures, especially humans. So, whatever the flash was, it was fucken quick for me not to pick it up.

After watching for a few more moments, I turn from the window. I try to relax, knowing after everything that's happened tonight, I'm not thinking clearly. Having the woman in the next room is not fucking helping the situation either. Taking a few steadying breaths, I glance at my old black leather lounge. I may as well get comfortable. It's going to be a long night trying to stop my body from wanting to enter the bedroom and fuck her hard while sinking my teeth into her pearly white skin, branding her and making her mine forever.

Chapter Five

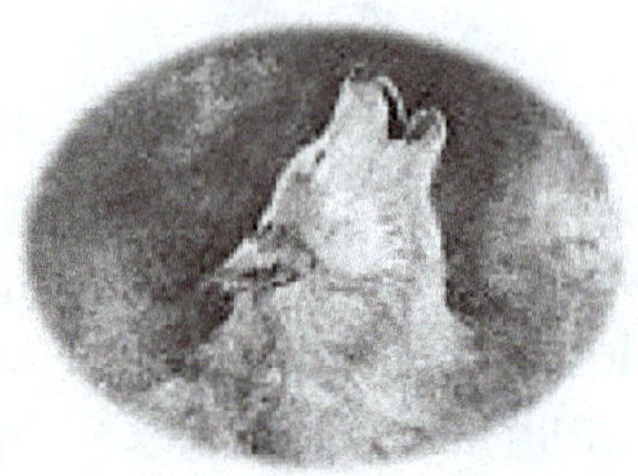

Emerson

I wake with a dull throbbing in the back of my head. Pressing my fingers to the base of my skull, I feel a small, crusty bump. I assume it's dry blood. What the hell happened to me? *Think Em.* I blink my eyes open, but hurriedly close them again when streams of sunlight hit my sensitive orbs. Rolling to one side, I bury my head in the pillow and drag the blankets up tight around me while cursing myself for not closing the blinds last night. Sucking in a deep breath, a scent of.... I don't know what it is, but it's alluring and assaults my senses, has my body humming with need. It's overpowering, all encompassing. *What is that smell?* Slowly pushing up onto my elbows, I use the back of my hand to wipe sleep from my eyes. A dull throb assaults my head and I try again to peel open my heavy lids.

Craning my head around, I take in the unfamiliar bedroom and push into a sitting position. I pat the other side of the bed making sure no-one is there. Why the hell am I not in my room at home? *Breath deep, Em,* I chant over and over as the dull throb forms into a pulsating smack at the base of my skull. Bringing fingers to my temples, I massage the spot and attempt to recall what happened last night. The last thing I remember is leaving the falls and then those eyes. The beautiful haunting eyes of my dreams, starring deep into my soul and captivating it. I must have passed out shortly after because I don't remember anything else. Lifting the bedcovers from my sleep stiff body, I praise a higher being, I'm still fully dressed.

Pushing the blankets off, I swing my legs over the edge of the massive four poster bed. I'm sure it's bigger than normal, it seems to swallow me. My feet dangle over the sides and only the tips of my toes brush the wooden boards. Sliding off the edge, a shiver races through my body as my bare feet touch the cold floor. Pushing to my feet, I stretch my aching muscles and head to the window. It's floor to ceiling glass over one complete side of the room. Peering out, I see how damn high I am up. The blue skyline, dotted with clouds along with the tops of trees, floods my vision and my stomach summersaults. I'm definitely not a fan of heights. "Don't look down, Em, don't look down." My attention is caught, the fear subsides. The most beautiful trees I have ever seen wrap around this side of the house, the color captures me and takes my mind off how high up in the air I am.

Turning away, I peruse the room. Gorgeous is the only way to describe it. Exposed wooden walls, high ceiling and a beautiful four poster bed flanked by matching bedside tables. To my right are two doors and I cross the room to the first one. I open the wood door and step into a closet large enough for two, but obviously used by only one person. To one side t-shirts hang neatly, jeans are folded and stacked on shelves, a pair of hiking boots lay scattered on the floor. I close the door and move to the second one. It opens into a beautiful bathroom which looks like something out a woodland retreat magazine. Stunning comes to mind, crisp and clean with an airy feel. Tan granite countertops and gold fixtures tie everything together.

Looking up, I note the ceiling is made of glass. Oooh, I can imagine laying back, relaxing in the sumptuous wooden bath and watching stars dance across the night sky. *Fuck what is wrong with me? I don't know where the hell I am and I'm planning my nights here. I think I hit my head harder than I thought.*

~

A throat clears, or was it a low growl behind me? I jump and swing around, a hand over my chest. I don't know why I assumed no-one else would be here. My heart skips a beat, no, I think it actually stops when my eyes meet the massive frame of a man leaning against the door frame. With one arm stretched above his head, I notice the flex of his muscles, the other hangs casually by his side. Studying his body from under my thick black lashes, I note every inch of the man's huge, heart stopping frame. Blue, low slung jeans pull tight around his muscled thighs and I lick my lips when I notice the button open at the top. His V-shape travels down, disappearing into the unknown. A snail trail of hair leads upward to his tanned six pack; his wide chest is decorated with tattoos which seem to flow over his broad shoulders. I swear he stands a little straighter as my eyes devour him. I drag my eyes away from his chest, my mouth is drier than a desert. I lift my eyes to his face, note his hard jaw where a slight tick thumps out a regular beat. Raising my eyes, they lock onto his and my breath leaves me as the liquid color drinks me in. I swear I see a flash of hunger and need behind those exquisite eyes. My body tunes into his and flashes like lightning run rampant through me. I clench my legs together to dull the ache as my thighs quiver, my breathing spikes matching the rapid beat of my heart. Watching him studying me, out of control feelings bombard my body. I don't know how, or why, this man has this effect on my body or why such emotions reach to the very pit of my stomach. I notice the uneven rise and fall of his chest and wonder if I'm having the same effect on him.

~

Clearing my throat and squaring my shoulders, I gaze into his eyes and hope my emotions are not showing on my face. He's turning my body to liquid and setting my ovaries on fire. He takes a few steps into the room and approaches where I'm standing in the bathroom. "Excuse me, but who are you?" I clear my throat again and hope the next time I speak; my voice will be stronger. I still don't know where the hell I am or who the heck this sex on legs is.

His eyes appear to soften and twinkle as he takes a moment to mull the question over. He takes the last few steps until he is standing in the doorway and places both of his huge hands on either side of the door frame, boxing me in. I can't help but stare as his muscles flex and contract. I feel the need to retreat, but push my shoulders back and stand my ground.

He looks deep into my eyes, a stare reaching all the way to my soul. Setting liquid heat so fierce running through me, I know my skin probably has a red tinge to it. The air seems to thicken around us and I experience a pull to him like nothing I have ever felt before. My brain seems to choose this moment to take a vacation, I watch as my arm reaches out and I drift the tips of my fingers down his chest. His skin is hot and sparks travel through me like a live wire. A hiss escapes his lips, but my focus remains where my fingers are resting. I feel the warmth of his hand as it engulfs mine and one word slips free from his lips on a growl. "Mine"

23

That one word settles deep inside me. One simple touch has me closing my eyes. Flashes and visions play out in my head making me gasp. My soul seems to shift and meld with his. Is this what my mother meant when she said, *one day you'll meet the man who will trigger your powers.* "Me?"

"Yes. I'm yours and you're mine."

On hearing the deep gravel of his voice, I snap my eyes to his. He winks and a sexy as sin grin pulls at his pouty lips. I want to bite them so badly. Instead, I sink my teeth into my bottom lip. I nod, knowing what he is saying is true because I can feel it.

Chapter Six

Raff

I heard her feet hit the floor and came to give her some aspirin for the headache I suspected she'd have after last night. All rational thought left my mind the moment she turned and those piercing blue eyes reeled me into her aura. The way her eyes studied every inch of me had me on high alert. My body reacted the only way it knew how, animal like, full of wolf like feelings and carnal need to claim her. As he tried claw his way out and into her petite body, I felt my skin giving way. But, I couldn't and wouldn't allow it just yet, my mate is not ready.

The way she eye fucked me caused my thinking to waiver for a split second as my already hard cock pushed against the zipper, aching to be released. The tips of her fingers as they feathered my chest, imprinted her into my skin and transported me to another place entirely. I closed my eyes and fought the urge to take her, slowly breathing as the sensations took me on a ride of arousal mixed with ownership.

When I wrapped my hand around her delicate fingers, was the moment our souls aligned. And, even if the right thing to do was to push her away, I can't. She's a part of me now, we're joined as one. If she were to leave me, I'd willingly accept the blade to cut my black heart from this soulless body. I'd be nothing without her by my side.

Her eyes flutter closed and a force stronger than I have ever known, surrounds us. I grip the door frame to remain upright, my knuckles turn white and my giant frame trembles. I don't know how I remain standing, I was convinced I would crumble to my fucking knees before her. She has something within, a strange pull which captures you and hangs on. I want to dig under her sweet exterior and find out what lurks under her snow-white skin. Fuck! This woman is going nowhere until I confirm what my body is saying - that she's my mate and imprinting on her is what I have to do.

~

Not being able to hold back any longer, my hands curl under her ass and I lift her into my arms. A squeal escapes her plump, pink lips and she wraps her legs around my waist. When I turn her toward the door frame, I feel the heat of her pussy rubbing against my aching cock. A rumble from deep in my throat escapes with my need to bury myself deep inside her.

I can't hold back and slam my mouth down on hers, craving her taste. I suck her small whimpers into my soul, claiming every one as mine. *Fuck, she tastes good. So much better than I'd imagined.* Ripping my mouth away from hers with a feral growl, my senses begin to overtake my self-control. I suck in deep breaths when I feel the heat from her fingertips dancing over my skin until she comes to the zipper of my jeans. Ever so fucking slowly, she eases it down. Anticipation of what's to come sets my blood on fire when she sets my throbbing cock free. I can't seem to stop her, nor do I fucking want to. I am overwhelmed with the need for another taste. Taking her bottom lip into my mouth, I suck and nibble, craving everything she has to give me. She wraps her hand around me and strokes my aching cock causing me to shudder when her skin touches mine. *Fuck, I need her naked now.*

Placing her back on her feet, I rid her of clothes before lifting her back into my arms. My cock brushes her entrance and I hiss at the contact.

"I need in you," I growl. All coherent thought has left me with the need to be inside this beautiful woman.

She nods her agreement to my silent question.

Reaching down, I brush the hard head of my cock against her, coating it in wetness while driving myself crazy with need. Pulling back a little, I line myself up and with one hard thrust I seat myself deep inside her hot pussy. A growl tears free when her inner muscles squeeze tight around me.

"Fuck." She feels like home. I thrust in and out, slow at first so she can adjust to my size. Then, I swivel my hips, hitting my mark and her muscles contract around me again.

"Right there," she pants as I thrust in harder and faster, pushing deep inside.

"Mine," I growl. I feel the orgasm crash over her hard and her body shudders with release. My teeth ache and lengthen. I latch onto the pure white silky skin in the pit of her collarbone and bite down, branding her as mine forever. Licking the small wound, I lave it with saliva sealing her fate.

"Yes, yours!" She screams out as her body tenses, readying for a second orgasm. She arches in my arms, pushing her breasts toward me. I latch onto one of her rosy colored nipples and after nipping the pebbled skin, plant tiny bites on the soft skin surrounding it. She hisses and shouts as another orgasm races through her. Her muscles contract around me like a vice and she takes me over the edge with her. A deep carnal growl echoes through the forest as my seed spills inside her.

~

Breathing hard, I lean my forehead against hers. Her soft pants whisper against my face, her eyes flutter open and the piercing blue hits me straight in the chest again. I know now, she is mine forever. Seeing my mating mark turns my cock rock hard again. I trace the indent with a finger and a soft hum of satisfaction leaves her lips. Staring deep into her eyes, I gather her closer, the light sheen of sweat coating her skin dampens my fingers. I sense her happiness and it satisfies a need deep inside me. I run my tongue across her lips and she gasps, opening to me. Taking her bottom lip between my teeth, I bite down and feel the pouty sweet flesh pop. Then, the metallic tang of her blood soaks the tip of my tongue. Our bodies move to the beat of our now mated hearts, shifting together as I take us on another orgasmic ride. I slide my lips across hers and kiss, lick and suck my way toward the pulse point behind her ear before licking the salt of her neck. I'm on the verge of coming undone inside her once more when a shrill scream pierces the air, shock waves of echo cut through the forest and deep into my bones.

My body freezes, all motion stops, I'm on instant alert. I sense my eyes changing no matter how hard I fight to prevent it. I'm transforming, powerless to stop it. I gaze deep into Emerson's eyes and the need to protect her overwhelms me. I cease fighting the change, I won't allow anything to harm her.

Sinking deep into her eyes, I mouth, "baby, I'm sorry." After brushing a swift kiss over her lips, I jump back into the open space of my room before dropping onto all fours. As the wolf I am appears, I glance back to my mate. She is surrounded by a glow and appears to be floating before me. Tilting my head back, I emit a loud howl. I'm trying to understand what the hell is happening, but the unease from last night washes over me and I run from the room. When I pounce from the back steps to the ground, I come face to face with someone I haven't seen in a very long time. My hair bristles, her eyes glow red. *What the fuck is happening?*

I posture and growl.

~

She flicks her wrist and instantly I'm in human form again. I don't give a fuck that I'm standing naked, but I do want to know why the fuck, Carly is standing before me.

Carly is a woman from my hometown in New Zealand. We were friends, but when she pushed for more I cut ties with her. I knew she wasn't my true mate and there was no point taking things further. To say she took it bad, is a fucken understatement. She didn't understand, I couldn't force something that would never fucking be. Putting the past aside, I need an answer to my question - why the fuck is she here and how the fuck did she find me? Nobody knows where I am except my brother, Frost, and some of our pack brothers.

"What the fuck are you doing here?" I attempt to hold back my anger, but her eyes narrow. Swirls of orange and red mist swirl as her eyes blacken, a ring of red around the edges appears. "What the fuck do you want?" I cross my arms over my broad chest.

"I want what's meant to be mine, YOU! You should never have pushed me aside, you were and always will be -

mine." Her growling voice is deathly low and a sadistic smirk spreads across her mouth causing the hairs on my arms to stand on end. "You will suffer for what you've done." She takes a step closer toward me and instinct forces me to step back.

"Suffer, for what?" I raise an eyebrow at her. *This bitch is crazy.*

"You tossed me aside like I was nothing, broke the part of me which should have stayed locked away in my black soul. It's your fault I'm here and like this. Yours and hers!"

She points to the tree house and the silhouette of my mate standing against the large glass windows. She is dressed in her sundress with the rays of dusk coming through the window behind her, lighting her soul like a blood orange halo.

"You were supposed to spend an eternity in hell as I was. It was all going to plan until you branded her!" She screams.

I turn back to face Carly as she raises her arm toward me and at that moment, the past crashes back into me. Visions of that fateful day, the accident which took my best friend's life, fill my mind. Then, thoughts of every bad event since that day when I'm around anyone. Realization hits with the force of a sledgehammer and the air leaves my lungs. This bitch has done something to me, a curse which causes me to hurt those who come close. "It was you, you did this to me!"

She nods and laughs like a woman possessed. The bitch is crazy.

"The day you walked away, I placed a curse on you. I never imagined you would find a way to break it, but I can fix that. It's why I'm here."

A soul piercing scream from my mate, the sound of shattering glass and darkness descends upon me. Not even my powers can save me now.

Chapter Seven

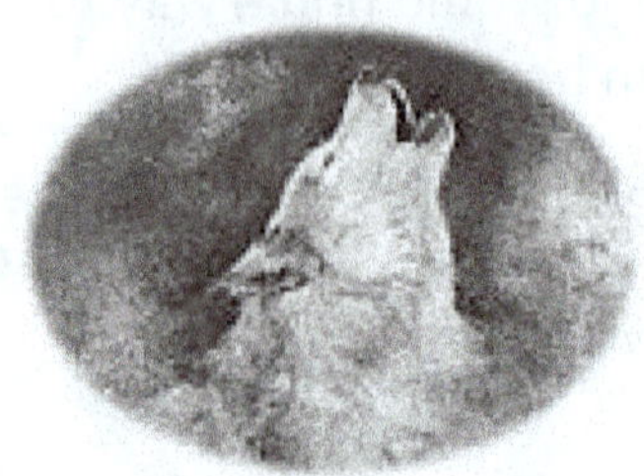

Emerson

I stand by the window, watching the scene below. I saw what was going to happen here, it flashed before me, in the forefront of my mind's eye. For the first time in my life, I feel whole. My mother said the true Emerson was buried deep inside, needing a kiss from my true soul mate to be released. Raff's kiss brought the real me to the surface, awakened me. This bitch thinks she can come here and take it all away from me? Fuck, NO! I don't think she realizes who and what I am. I have already lost one family, they were taken from me because I didn't see what was coming. I sure as shit am not losing Raff now I've finally found him. The moment his teeth broke the skin on my neck, I knew what he was. A burning sensation assaulted my body as the venom of wolf hit my bloodstream and his saliva sealed him deep inside my soul forever.

~

I grew up in a small town with wolf shifters, my great-grandmother found her soul mate with a wolf. It is said, once the soul finds the one person they are supposed to be with, all their powers and shifting ability come to life. My mother would tell me the story of how I came from a long line of seers, that it missed a generation with her. We thought it had also missed me, but I guess we were wrong.

The whole town thought it was my fault when my parents died in a car accident. It wasn't a secret who my family was, and the townfolk believed I was hiding my powers to protect myself. When I met Daniel, my ex, I hoped he was the key to unlock everything within me. It turned out I was wrong. The slime ball was jumping anyone he could find and I was too fucking naive and stupid to see what was right in front of my eyes. I was too busy living inside my head, thinking my life was complete. Ignoring the true form my grandmother said had always lived inside me.

~

I hear the rumble of thunder echo above me, breaking into my thoughts. Glancing up, I see dark clouds rolling in and the first drops of rain fall to the earth. Turning toward the waterfall, I watch as water crashes over the rocks; a brilliant kaleidoscope of colors flash over the diamond like surface and I know what I have to do next. Closing my eyes, I feel the air whipping around me, lifting me off my feet. I hover through the window and descend slowly to the ground, landing on the tips of my toes as a puff of air billows around me in a smoky haze. Mesmerized, my breath whooshes out, for the first time in a very long tormenting time I can feel them, the embrace of my family I so foolishly thought I had lost. A sweet sound kisses my ears as my Grandma, my mentor's voice comes through like summertime rain. Closing my eyes, I savor this feeling of belonging as she whispers her words of wisdom....

"Sweet Emerson, push through the walls you erected so long ago, let the mist from the falls guide you through the hurt."

Feeling like a weight has been lifted from my shoulders, I let her words soothe me. Then, an evil laugh penetrates my senses and I snap my eyes open to stare at the one Raff called, Carly. My eyes drift over her, studying my enemy. Petite in size, she's dressed in what looks like the uniform worn by the staff at the small café I visit in the mornings before work. Her hair is black as night streaked with red. Her eyes are the darkest I have ever seen. I stiffen. This woman has served me time and time again at the café and she always gave me an uneasy feeling as she is now. Her eyes seem to sharpen and penetrate me to my very core. I ignore the uneasy feeling washing over me and glance down at Raff laying on the ground. He's in pure wolf form, not moving at all and at that moment, I know I'll do anything to bring him back to me.

"He is lost for eternity and nothing you do will change that." She cackles as if reading my mind.

I glare at her and can't help the pity I feel swelling inside me. I easily push it a side when I remember, she is the reason Raff is not moving right now. I match her sadistic smile with one of my own.

"Bitch, please. You have no idea who I am, do you?" My tone is cold as ice. She should know this is far from over and I'm not backing down, no matter what. "You have someone who belongs to me and believe me, I *will* get him back!"

She rolls her eyes and flicks her nails like I'm boring her, a sick smile forms over her ugly features.

"Darling, so sorry to disappoint you, but that won't be happening in this lifetime or the fucken next." She speaks as if I'm being delusional.

I have a strange feeling in my stomach, the rain falls heavier now and I turn to the waterfall. The diamond mist rises off the water in the shape of a wolf and my heart picks up speed. I feel the ripples slice under my skin and my nails begin to ache. I close my eyes as I feel myself shift, breaking from the bounds which have held me for what has felt like an eternity. It's freeing, bones crunch, teeth grate as the true Emerson comes to life.

~

Blinking my eyes open, everything slams into me at once. The sharp smell of the forest, the sparkle of the waterfall so bright it's almost blinding. I spin toward Carly and note the red death stare she is shooting my way. Hackles rise along my back and my fangs are bared when she raises her hand to me. I assume she wants to do to me what she has done to Raff, but I'm quicker and see it coming. I growl furiously, leap into the air and latch onto her arm. Her blood curdling scream echoes around us. She lifts her leg, kicks out and connects with my back legs. It forces me to release her and I fall to the ground, a cloud of dust swirls around me.

Shaking out my fur, I snap my head toward where Raff lays still as stone. Fuck, what the hell do I do? I spin back to where the evil bitch is, but she's no longer there. Crawling on all fours, I search the immediate area. She's nowhere to be seen, but couldn't have disappeared that fast into thin fucken air. Pushing my body up from the ground, I listen and hear the sounds of running, the slight snap and crack of twigs and dry leaves coming from the patch of trees behind me. I jump in front of Raff's body as a blinding red and orange light flashes before me. A strange warmth, mixed with the cool kiss of the cold, overtakes my body and an aurora of lights swirls around us both.

Lowering to my knees, I shift back into my human form and lay my head on my mate's chest. A humming sensation settles deep in my belly when I feel the vibration of his deep husky voice over my cheek calling my name. My eyes lock with his liquid pools. He reaches out and runs his fingers lightly over my cheek before whispering in a deep sexy voice which has butterflies swimming in my belly

"My Beauty."

Chapter Eight

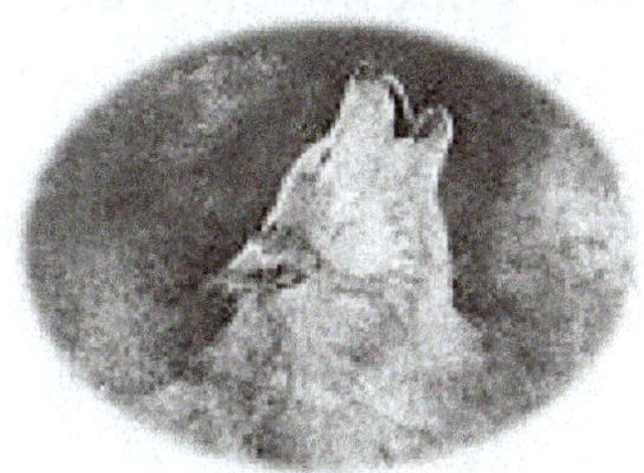

Raff

I feel like I'm floating, yet I'm not moving. Pure fucking blackness surrounds me. I have no way of knowing how long I've been here. I feel a strong presence around me, like invisible strings are pulling at me like a puppet master and his doll. My mind drifts between the past and present. After all this time, I now realize I've been cursed by a demon dressed as a woman. A woman who said she loved me, who pleaded with me not to leave and to make her mine. I lost my best friend, left my pack because of that damn fucken curse and all this time, I thought it was me. How did I not figure it out sooner, put the shattered pieces together when it all started to unravel into this dark nightmare? For the past year I have struggled with the beast I thought lived deep inside me as he tried to claw to the surface. I know I wasn't born this way, it happened after I told Carly my heart could never love her for my soul couldn't imprint on a lie. She is the reason I have felt like the beast was overtaking me, her curse made me believe it's who I really was on the inside.

Carly is a demon, it all makes sense now. It's crystal clear to me and will soon be to my brothers. My mind is muddled right now, but the explanation is clear. I ask again, how did I not realize this before? She must have followed me here because no-one from my old pack would tell her where I was, especially not my brother. That would mean she's been watching me for far longer than I've been here. *Fucking bitch!* I need to find a way out of this darkness, but how? I feel a presence again, pulling at me and instead of trying to fight it, I let go and float toward it.

~

I feel a warmth spread over me as refreshing drops of water hit my face. I'm in human form again, lying on the ground near the edge of the waterfall. The hypnotic sound of the water falling over the rocks brings me out of the fog. Something lands on my chest and I blink my eyes open. I look down to see a mop of inky black hair spread over me and the angelic face of my mate stares back at me, eyes as bright as crystals.

"My Beauty," I breath out. Reaching down, I caress her soft silky cheek with the rough pad of my thumb. A cough escapes me and I realize my voice is huskier than usual. My heart misses a beat when a smile spreads over her lips, but then her eyes close and I feel the weight of her body press down on me.

~

My ears prick up when I hear a rustling sound from the bushes on the other side of the waterfall. Carly emerges, staring at me with eyes as bright as fire.

"She sacrificed herself for you, how fucking noble." She glares at me, waiting until her words register. "Now you will live in that hell you deserve without your mate by your side."

I glance down at Emerson, her breathing is shallow, her pulse slow.

"Fuck, no!" I sit up and pull her closer into my chest hoping my heated skin will help in some way, warm her cooling body which with each passing second is turning ice cold. Wrapping a protective arm tight around my mate, I hold her close to my side. It's as if she was made to fit. My eyes stay fixed on Carlys as she stalks toward us, a sinful smirk gracing her lips. I shuffle back so she can't close the distance between us and get her hateful hands near my girl. The ground shifts underneath me and we are falling into the crisp water surrounding the waterfall. I hold Emerson closer, not willing to lose her to the water. After what feels like falling forever, I realize there is no point living if I can't have her by my side so, I open my eyes and look at my girl one more time before allowing the water to take us both.

~

My eyes grow heavy as oxygen leaves my body. As my lids drift shut on the best day I've ever had, I feel a feather-light touch against my face. Using what strength I have left, I peel my eyes open. The vision before me has my chest tightening and it's not from the lack of oxygen or the water, it's a pair of piercing crystal blue eyes and a glowing aura surrounding my mate. She leans in and places her lips over mine. That one touch has my lungs filling as we share the air. At this point in time, we're in a bubble of our own, surrounded by the crashing of the waterfall. Gripping my hand, she turns and glides through the water with ease, pulling me with her as we glide to the edge.

Chapter Nine

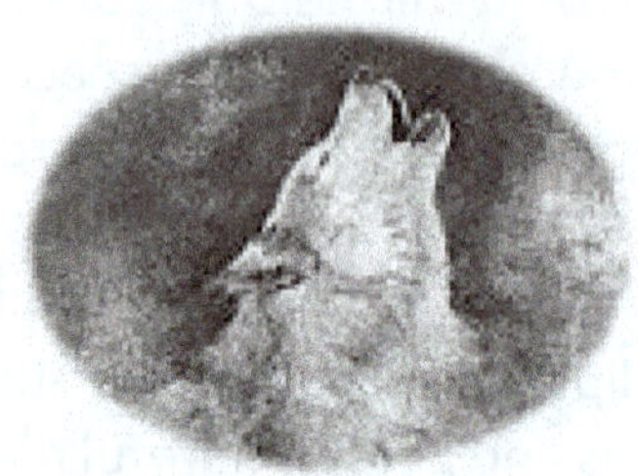

Emerson

Sacrificing myself for him was as easy as breathing. There was no doubt, or hesitation, about taking her fire. Falling into him and hearing his voice murmur one last time as the fire of his touch licked over my skin, I knew I was home and this time I had saved who could have been the love of my life. Slipping into darkness, I knew what was coming next and I wasn't scared. I'll never be scared again. He was my light, if only for a little while. Raff showed me what living was all about though I sensed darkness holding him back. He gave me something to treasure until the very end. With these thoughts running through my head, I let the darkness wrap around me like an old coat and picture the sexy smile playing on his lips while his liquid eyes glow for me. Off in the distance, I hear murmured voices and feel the warmth of his arms as I drift away.

~

My body tingles, my senses kick in and I hear Gramma's voice telling me to draw strength in and don't give up. "Drink the water, let it consume you, heal you and make you stronger." Her voice echoes through the crashing of the falls, a sound I know so well. I wiggle my toes, open my mouth and swallow the diamond water I have admired for so long. As it slides down my throat I feel my strength begin to return. Drawing on the strength from generations past, I push through the remaining darkness and then I see him. The same sensations and emotions wash over me as the first time I was this close to him. Reaching forward, I run my fingers down the side of his face feeling the beginning of stubble covering his hard jaw. I gaze into his eyes, emerald chips sparkle brightly against the backdrop of liquid lead. I press my lips to his and share the air in my lungs while we're cocooned in a bubble of white hot lust sending off star bursts behind my eyes. Pulling my lips from his, I open my eyes and feel the loss of connection, but we need to leave the water and finish what has been started.

~

After helping Raff's weakened body to the water's edge, I stand flick the hair from my face and lunge into the space where Carly is standing. A look of pure shock washes over her face.

"Yes, bitch. I'm back."

She steps back but before she has a chance to cast a spell over me, I grip the tops of her arms, halting her movements.

"I thought I'd killed you?" Her voice is laced with surprise.

"It didn't stick," I snap back sarcastically.

I release one hand and before she has a chance to blink, I wrap my fingers around her throat in a choke hold. Her eyes bug out as I grip tighter and my nails pierce the skin, restricting her air supply. Pleasure washes through me unlike anything I have ever felt before.

I hear Raff get to his feet and worry he may try to intervene. This is my fight now so, I turn my head, narrow

41

my eyes and order him to, "stay." The word comes out on a low growl, rolling from the back of my throat.

He stares at me for a moment and must see I need to do this, I need to take care of this situation. When he winks at me, a sexy smirk dances on his lips then, he nods his head in understanding.

Returning my focus back to Carly, I glare into her burning red eyes and feel mine ignite with red hot heat. "Thought you had won, sweetheart?" I growl. "Well, you guessed wrong."

Whipping my hand down fast, I drop to one knee and slam her body over my thigh. Her back arches over my muscle and she opens her mouth to scream, but with my grip tight on her windpipe and my fingers crushing her voice box, only a gurgling sound can be heard. I wrap a fist full of hair around my hand and snap her head back, exposing the taut skin of her neck. Carnal need surges within me, a need to finish what she started, but not having it end the way she wanted. Peeling back my lips allows my canines to grow to full length and I see the fear flash in her eyes. "You lose, bitch." Terror distorts her face when I lean down and sink my canines into her jugular, ripping her throat out.

~

I feel the dead weight of her body fall over my leg as the life leaves her and push her to the ground. After wiping blood soaked hands on my dress, I stand and step over her body as if in a daze. I lower to my knees and take deep breaths of cool air into my burning lungs to calm myself down.

My head snaps up at the sound of footsteps off to one side, my eyes lock on Raffs. I watch as he makes his way toward me, stepping into my space. Leaning forward, he runs the pads of his fingers across my mouth wiping Carly's blood from my lips before capturing my lips in a soft kiss. His tongue prods at the seam of my lips, I gasp and grant him access, allowing him to take my mouth in a deep kiss which sends sparks racing through my body. Sweeping me into his arms, I lock my ankles around his waist and he carries me back to the water's edge before placing me on my feet.

"Sit babe, I'll be back."

I do as he asks, letting my feet dangle in the diamond water. Glancing skyward, I notice the rain has stopped and the clouds are drifting away. A beautiful rainbow pokes through and arches over the falls.

I turn to see Raff descending the stairs, naked as the day he was born. My body trembles as tingles shoot off in all directions. I watch as he approaches Carly's body, mesmerized by his graceful movement. I notice the matches and a tin can in his hand. Opening the top, he pours liquid over her and strikes a match, dropping the burning red flame onto her body. I'm transfixed as I watch bright blue and orange flames leaping upward.

I don't see my mate come back to me or, slide into the water before me, but I do feel him push my legs apart, wrap his arms around my waist and rest his head in my lap. Dragging me from my trance, I gaze down at him and run my fingers through his thick hair. The vibration of his hum of satisfaction spreads through me. Lifting his face in my hands, I lean down and press a soft kiss to his lips before murmuring what I feel my soul has known since the minute we met, "I love you."

Taking a deep breath, he takes my lips in a hard kiss and drags me forward until we're entwined in each other's arms and floating through the diamond water as the majestic waterfall crashes down around us.

"I love you, too."

Chapter Ten

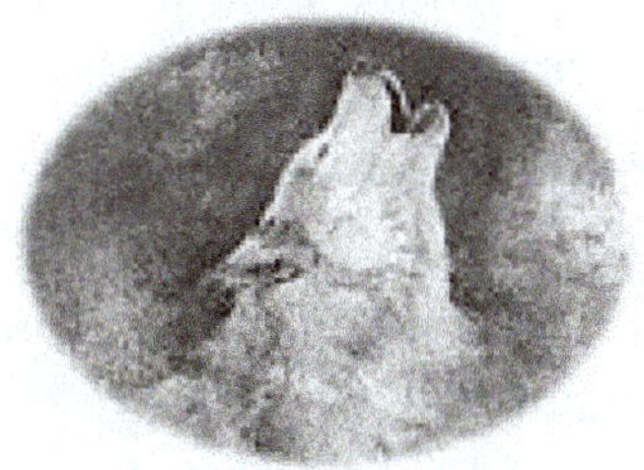

Raff

Sucking down the sounds rising from deep in her throat, I claim her lips as mine. It's as if I can't get enough. Running my hands down her back, I grip the material of her dress in both hands, clench it tight in my fists and in one swift movement, rip it wide open exposing the overheated skin I need to touch as my body screams out for the contact. She gasps and growls into my mouth before taking her hands from my hair and ridding herself of what's left of the material. Leaning into me, her hard nipples rub against my chest and her fingers return to fisting my hair. She tilts her neck to the side and I trace an invisible line with my tongue toward the pulse point behind her ear. She fists my hair tighter and when a moan falls from her lips, I suck it into my mouth.

Feeling her heart beating against me settles the churning of knots in my stomach. I thought I'd lost my forever before it truly began. Having her in my arms with her legs locked around me as we float through the majestic falls, has my body burning with carnal need. I want to mark her over and over so, there is no doubt in her mind - she is mine.

~

"Fuck me," she gasps into my ear before her teeth latch onto the lobe and bite down with enough force to send my arousal skyrocketing.

I slide her body down mine, turn and push her against the rock wall behind the waterfall. We create our own bubble as the water blankets us from the bright sun. Bracing my arms against the wall on either side of her head, I devour her mouth, addicted to her taste. She draws back and loses focus when she notices a hidden alcove beside us, an alcove with its own mysteries waiting inside.

Leaning forward, I lick my mating mark and push my hard cock through her wet folds to bring her back to the moment. Sliding deep inside her, she moans. I groan at the tightness of her inner walls, accepting me, squeezing, pulsating, clenching around my hard length. I suck in a deep breath and compose myself, I don't want to lose control now. I want this burnt into her sweet soul forever. Gazing into her blue eyes, I see the need there, but silver flecks seem to illuminate the shadows. I thrust slow at first until her body strains and pushes for more.

"Faster," she pants.

I will never deny my beautiful mate anything. Picking up my pace, I hiss and arch into her nails as they scrape down my back. A deep, throaty growl leaves me when I feel her teeth latch onto my chest, branding me with her mark.

"Fuck, Beauty," I groan. "What you do to me." I thrust harder and take her lips in a bruising kiss. Her legs tense up around my thighs and I know she is close, so close I feel the orgasm rippling around me, but I need to hear her say it again before I let her fall over the edge.

"Say it," I demand slamming into her as a moan falls from her lips. I stare into her heavy, hooded eyes and fuck me, it's almost enough to send me crashing over the edge. I grit my teeth, pushing past the need to fill her with my seed and breed her. *Fuck, breed her?* Where did that come from. I picture her round with my cubs and a surge of possessiveness washes over me. Fuck, I want that. I slam into her again, unable to stop as the image plays out in my mind. I slam in deeper as her moans and whimpers echo around us. I nip the lobe of her ear and growl again, "Say it." Easing back, I watch as pure ecstasy washes over her face. I need to hear it. Fuck, I need it bad.

"I love you," she whispers and arches her back against the wall. She takes what she wants and screams out, "I'm yours."

"Fuck yeah, you are," I grit out between clenched teeth. Slamming into her, we fall into a rhythm, giving and taking. It's sexy as fuck watching her take her pleasure from me. I slam into her fast and unforgiving, taking her body on a ride to the abyss of lust before spiraling back down, linked together now as a pack of one. The orgasm rips through me stronger than I have ever felt before. Overwhelming tremors assault her small frame. *What the fuck was that?*

~

After my mind-numbing orgasm, I regain my senses, lean down and rest my forehead against hers before planting a feather-light kiss to her swollen lips. I breathe into her mouth hoping it soaks deep into her soul. "I love you." And, because I need for her to hear it again, "you're mine."

Running her fingers through my hair with a dreamy satisfied look on her face, she nods her head in understanding and wraps her arms around my neck, resting her head against my chest completely boneless. I chuckle and kiss the top of her head. Staying inside her, I move us from under the waterfall and back into the now setting sun. I feel the mist from the fall hit my face and for the first time in a long time, I feel free of the darkness. I feel a sense of peace, because of this beauty in my arms who will be forever, MINE.

Pulling her deep into my body, I wrap my arms around her. With her head resting in the crock of my shoulder, I carry her from the crystal waters, leaving the diamond sheen of the majestic falls lacing our bodies. I gaze into the sleep filled eyes of my beautiful woman and lean forward to kiss the tip of her nose. "Let's take you home."

Looking up to the tree tops which hold the house I will now share with my mate, sends a quiver of belonging over me. I take the stairs two at a time until we reach the top. As the sun sets over the mountains, I lift her a little higher in my arms and grip her tighter. Her gaze meets mine and a smile plays across her lips. A smile I will never tire of. I smile back down at her and she mouths, "HOME."

My cock thickens and my heart rate spikes. That one word means more than any pack oath. I tilt my head back and send a soul consuming howl into the wind, to travel on its wings to my pack far away in my homeland. A sign I have made it out of the darkness, found my mate and imprinted, the way our spirit brothers before us had.

Turning with my mate in my arms we watch as the sun kisses goodnight to the moon. My mind travels to thoughts of the future and what we can do here in this magical place called Millaa Millaa Falls. Where legends live, stories are told and stories are yet to be written. A new era to form a new pack and start what we all long for - a family, a home and a sense of belonging. My brother Frost started a retreat for orphaned baby cubs which have either been abandoned or given up. I think something like that here would be perfect. With that thought in mind, I turn and stride to our master bedroom. Moving to the bed, I lay my mate down and watch as she rolls over, hugs the pillow and hums in satisfaction. As much as I want to lay with her in my arms, I need to call my brother and organize for him to send me one of the pack brothers to help. If my beauty falls pregnant with my cubs, I don't want her having to worry about anything other than resting.

Epilogue

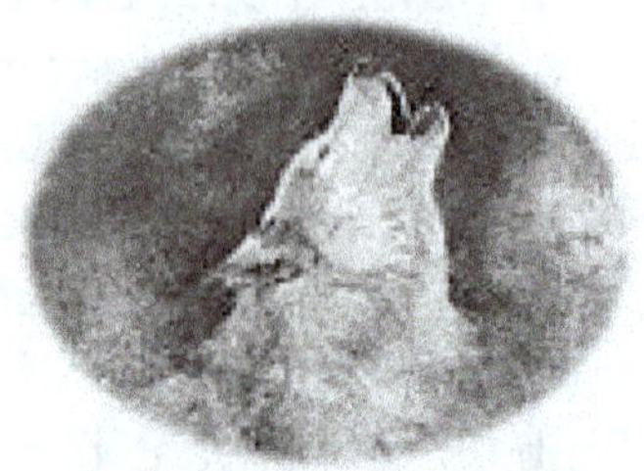

One week later...

Raff

Taking the stairs two at a time, I hurry over to the falls whose magic brought my mate home to me. I watch as a kaleidoscope of colors bounce off the glass like surface and notice how much brighter it looks today. This particular spot, where the sun hits the water sending up shards of rainbows, is Em's favorite place to visit. She said, this is where she feels her family the strongest, almost like she can reach out and touch them.

I used a few tree logs I'd found and built her a love seat near the water's edge. A stone path leads to our front steps, she can sit here overlooking the falls and her new home.

When it was finished, I waited until the sun began to kiss the sky for a new day. After blindfolding her, I grasped her hand and led her down the stone path. When we reached the seat, I turned her to face me and removed the blindfold. I whispered in her ear after brushing my lips over hers.

"Keep your eyes closed, baby."

She did as I asked and I turned her until her back rested against my chest, wrapped my arms around her waist and buried my nose in her hair. Before resting my chin on the top of her head, I took a moment to breathe in her intoxicating scent.

"Open your eyes my beauty."

A small gasp escaped her lips and her hands rose to her mouth, "Oh my God, Raff it's stunning." Amazement sounded clear in her voice and any doubt I had about her not liking the seat left me instantly. Turning in my arms, she locked eyes with me and the love within them blew my mind.

~

I feel myself hardening in my jeans when I remember the way she stared at me. Her eyes were filled with overwhelming love, lust and carnal need, all directed toward me. Muscles flex and my breathing becomes rapid when I feel the same need for her run through me now. Images of the first time I saw her shift assault my mind. The magnificent vision of her wolf form, caramel brown fur, bright silver eyes with piercing chips of sparkling blue knocked me to my knees. Her intoxicating beauty has nothing on my dark brown fur and green eyes.

Em insists my fur matches the magnificent color of the finest chocolate and my eyes are not only green, but sparkle like emeralds with specks of shimmering liquid lead. Whatever the fuck that means.

Whenever I shift, it's like my beauty's body comes to life and she can't get enough of me. So, the way she thinks about me must be a good thing. *Right?*

A chuckle leaves me when I remember how excited and happy she became when she first realized, when we are both shifted, we are able to read each other's minds. I explained to her, only true soul mates who are connected as one have this ability.

~

I shake my head to clear the images before my cock begins to ache. I glance toward the water, soaking in the knowledge that my woman's tears which once flowed into these waters, don't anymore. After she told me the story about losing her parents in a car accident, I shared my own story about losing my best friend, things began clearer for us after that. When I explained what had happened that night a year ago, I had seen the sadness in her eyes, I hated that I'd hurt her with my truth. But, to my surprise, she wrapped her arms around me and told me how much she loved me. I close my eyes against the sudden pain in my chest and take a few deep breaths. When the pain seems to ease, I look back to the water crashing over the rocks and remember that night again as if it was yesterday……

It was supposed to be a routine scout job, we would search the known drop spots where shifters were known to abandon their cubs. It turned into a disaster when lightning flashed around us and we became separated. I remember howling to gain my friend's attention, but he didn't answer. Further flashes of lightning assaulted my eyes leaving bright dots behind in their wake. I stumbled through the pelting rain as the rolling sound of thunder assaulted my ears. A fork of lightning hit the tree tops illuminating the clearing in front of me and my eyes locked onto my pack brother. I knew it was him, but I was in a haze of confusion. My body felt strange, possessed. I had no rational thought, no control and I lunged toward him, taking him to the ground. I shook my head, coming out of a daze as my human form re-emerged. Cold rain hit my bare skin, bringing me back to the present and the realization of what the fuck I'd done. I rushed to his side, frantically searching his form for a muscle twinge, a heartbeat, anything at all which would tell me he was still alive. Fuck! There was nothing, nothing but blood. When I realized I'd killed my best friend, I howled out a tortured cry. The same dazed and consuming feeling bombarded me again and before I knew what was happening, I had changed from the Raff I'd once been to a monstrous beast. Since that night, when anger, fear or pain ripped through me, the same haze would roll over me and I would lose control of myself. After I would wake and find myself naked in my human form with nothing but destruction surrounding me.

For the past year I have carried the guilt with me, but now I know it was something the bitch had done to me I don't blame myself anymore, but it still hurts like no fucken tomorrow. Knowing my best friend died by my hands tears me apart, but Emerson is helping me to push past the pain and come into the light.

I hear the rustling of trees behind me, twigs breaking as the sound of heavy footsteps approach. I swing around, instantly on high alert. My mind conjures up murderous thoughts. Hackles raise and my body edges toward shifting. My breathing calms when my eyes land on a wolf brother from New Zealand. The great Silas, travel weary with a bag slung low over his shoulder.

~

When I called my brother last week and told him of my plans to start a rescue retreat here in Millaa Millaa Falls, he was disappointed I had chosen to stay here but understood and was interested in helping me. He told me, pack brother Silas was looking to branch out and he would send him to me to help with whatever I needed. In return, I had to promise to visit with my new mate. It wasn't hard to convince her. Em's eyes lit up at the possibility of visiting where I'd been raised and to meet my brother and his new mate. I'd be lying if I said I wasn't looking forward to meeting the woman who had captured my brother's soul.

"Silas, so good to see you brother. How have you been?" I drag him into my arms and slap his back in greeting.

"Great, brother." He peers around and his eyes lock on the majestic waterfall behind me. I watch his eyes narrow and ears flinch.

I wonder what he is staring at, but when I swing around, I see only water crashing down and bright colors bouncing around in the mist.

"What's wrong?" I turn back toward him.

At the sound of my voice, his attention returns to me. Before he can answer, I hear the footsteps of my mate as she descends the steps. Looking toward her, I see the bright smile she shoots at Silas and growl low in my throat as jealousy spikes through me.

She turns to me and giggles. I don't think there is anything funny about this, she's mine and so is that smile.

"Oh hush, Raff," she says, waving her hand in the air. She moves beside me and wraps her arm around my waist.

My jealousy settles a little when she rests her head against my arm. As I start to introduce them, I see Silas' focus is back on the waterfall. I glance down at Emerson and watch a small smile curl her lips. I wonder what she's thinking about, but don't have the chance to ask.

"Why don't we go inside, I've just made lunch." She spins on her heel to head back to our home. Stopping a couple of feet away, she looks back to the waterfall with the

54

same smile as before on her face. She closes her eyes and breaths in the atmosphere she says calms her soul.

"Silas, is it?" She glances over her shoulder, eyebrows raised.

"Yes," his husky voice growls out at her.

"Magical, isn't it?" Em points toward the spot he was taken by less than five minutes ago. Not waiting for an answer, she starts toward the steps again.

Looking at Silas, I wonder if he knows what she is talking about, but he shakes his head at me. *I'll have to ask her what it's about later.* We follow a couple of feet behind my mate and I'm alarmed when I see her sway on her feet. When her foot slips from the step she was about to take and she begins to fall backward, I wonder what the fuck is happening. I'm there in flash and wrapping my arms around her, I hoist her up against my chest. My heart beats out of control when I look down to see her eyes are closed and she's passed out.

"Emerson!" I shout, but nothing. "Em, come on baby, wake up." Still nothing.

"What happened," Silas asks as he rushes to my side.

"Fuck, I don't know." Terror sweeps through me and I hold her closer. Pressing my fingers to the pulse point on her neck, I'm relieved to find her heart is beating like normal. "I need to get her into the house and lay her down on the bed. Then, I need to work out what the fuck just happened and hope to fuck she wakes up."

We enter the house and I head toward the sofa, Silas grabs a pillow from the armchair and I lower her onto it. As her head hits the pillow, her eyes flutter open. I blow out the breath I didn't realize I was holding and fall to my knees beside her. Reaching over, I trace my fingers down the side of her face.

"Are you okay, baby? You had me scared to death."

She nods and a smile teases her lips. Reaching out, she takes my hand, brings it to her belly and holds it there. I'm trying to figure out what the hell is happening when she speaks and my body is overcome with pure soul-crushing ecstasy.

"I'm pregnant."

~

Almost 4 months later...

Emerson

I run my hand over my growing belly and thank the powers above that wolves are only pregnant for four months and not the nine months like humans. I could handle it, but Raff certainly couldn't. Ever since the moment I held his hand to my belly and said the words - I'm pregnant - I swear he has become more overprotective with each and every day that passes. I had to stop working at the library two and half months ago because he wouldn't leave my side. I know how much work he has going on here so, I made the decision to be here with him. He can now focus on what he needs to do so our pack can be bigger and stronger. I silently thank Frost every day for sending Silas to us, he helps rein in Raff when he becomes more overprotective than usual.

Pushing to my feet I lean my hand on the back of the lounge for leverage to push myself the rest of the way up. Feeling steady on my feet, I walk, hmm walk isn't the right word, waddle would be more appropriate right now. I giggle to myself as I waddle toward the front door, I have a need to sit near the waterfall for a while. I reach for the door handle and hear a growl from behind me. I smile as the vibration runs through me.

"Beauty, where are you going?" Raff's deep voice rumbles from behind me as the heat of his body warms my back and his hand comes down over mine.

"I want to sit by the fall for a while." I turn into his embrace and gaze up through my thick dark lashes, allowing a pout to form on my lips. Since I became my true self I don't need my glasses anymore and the clarity of my eyes is on full display. Raff says my eyes did things to him before, but day by day they have even more of an effect on him. I try to use that to my advantage, like right now.

"Fuck, Beauty, don't look at me like that." He reaches up with his free hand and runs his thumb over my lips. "Come on I'll carry you out."

Before I can protest that I can walk, okay waddle outside by myself I'm up in his arms and cocooned against his hard chest. He opens the door and descends the stairs, heading to my carved wooden seat. Placing me down, I run my finger over the small plaque he had made for me.

"For my Beauty, my Life, my Light, my Mate."

Bending down, Raff slides a finger under my chin, brings my face up to his and brushes a soft kiss over my lips "I'll be back soon, baby." I nod and watch as he heads back towards home. Instead of heading inside, he walks over to Silas in the garden beneath our home. Peeling my eyes off my man when he rips his shirt off, I remind myself that he needs to help Silas not cater to my hormones right now. Feeling flushed, I look toward the diamond water and soak in the atmosphere surrounding it. I try to think of anything other than my man and his rippling muscles right now.

~

My grandmother and past generations slip into my thoughts and I smile remembering the power which surrounded us for a long time. I explained what I could remember to Raff about the stories told to me as a child and he seemed as captivated as me.

My great-grandmother was raised by her mother and aunties who were powerful witches. She was told, when she met her soulmate that different powers would arise. Those powers could be of love, the power to control the elements or to see into the future. When my great-grandmother met her soulmate, she learned he was a wolf. It had never been heard of, a wolf and a witch joining as one, but nothing could tear them apart and once they were joined at the soul and she wore his mate mark, something magical happened. When they conceived their first child, my grandmother, she received the ultimate gift of being able to shift into a wolf and also to see into the future once she met her soulmate. But, my grandmother's soulmate turned out to be a human and so the magic which consumed her never passed to my mother. When I was born my grandmother said I was born with an aura around me and she knew once I meet my soul mate, I would discover the true me. I couldn't understand why my mother didn't receive powers, but my grandmother said nobody is sure why some people gain them and some don't. And now, rubbing my hand over my belly I know my cubs will be the ultimate strong chain with Witch, Wolf shape shifting and the power to see glimpses into the future. I couldn't be more excited to meet them.

In the space of four short months it seems I have everything I ever dreamed about. The only piece missing is my parents, but they're the reason I love to sit by the diamond water. It gives me a sense of feeling them, in me, beside me. I feel closer to them just by being here.

I watch the water crash over the rocks and see a flicker of purple from the dark alcove behind the fall, the same flicker I saw the day Silas arrived. I smile and hope she will make herself known very soon and take his soul, not only his dreams.

~

A rolling pain stabs at my belly and another shoots into my back. I'm unsure of what it could be. Surely, it couldn't be labor, I have another two weeks. The pains hit again, sharper and longer this time. I hiss and try to push myself onto my feet, it takes a moment, but I eventually stand and start to pace back and forth. My body seems to know what it is doing and panting begins. I breathe in deeply, blow out slowly as sweat pools at my spine and a light sheen forms on my forehead. I lean forward, brace my hands on the bench and squeeze my eyes shut against a scream which tries to escape. I bite down hard on my lip, the copper taste of blood drips lightly on my tongue.

I glance over my shoulder to where Raff is helping Silas in the garden, I know I need to call out to him. I can't hold back the ear-piercing scream and call out my mate's name as excruciating pain takes over my body. I sway my hips from side to side, trying to keep control, but it's no use. The wolf within pushes forward and takes over, emitting a painful howl to our mate.

Dropping to all fours, my back arches and I howl as another contraction hits me. Once it subsides, I glance up through watery eyes and see my mate and his friend running toward me and shouting. I'm in too much pain to understand a word they are saying. I close my eyes and try to steady my breathing as I feel our babies trying to push themselves into the world. I open my eyes to find Raff running his hand through my sweaty fur, pushing it from my eyes. A look of disbelief mixed with happiness swims in his eyes.

Another contraction ripples through me and a soul shattering howl escapes me. Raff shifts and circles me before coming to lay by my side, he licks my face soothingly.

"I don't know if I can do this." Whimpers leave my mouth.

"You can, baby." He leans over and nuzzles me. "Fuck, you are so beautiful."

He's trying to keep the worry from his eyes, but I see it and wish I could ease his concerns, but right now, I'm in too much bloody pain. From the corner of my eye, I notice Silas pacing. I jump and whimper when Raff sends out a warning growl not to come near me. His eyes shift from Raff to me before he nods his head and takes a few steps back.

"Beauty, you need to push now."

I hope I give him a go fuck yourself wolf look and snap, "I don't need to do a fucking thing."

His mouth opens as if on a smile and his ears flick up at my tone. It irritates me further as pressure builds and the urge to push overcomes me. Laying down on my side, I do what my body wants. I allow the pain and pressure to overtake me and push with all I have. Once, twice, three times and then relief, as my first pup covered in dark fur comes into the world. A whimper leaves me again as the roll of pain continues and the pressure builds. Four mighty pushes later and pup number two has arrived, also covered in dark hair like his father I barely have time to breathe before pup number three erupts into the world with a howl. Her coat is pure white. I watch as Raff licks them clean and guides them to my breasts to feed. They moan and cry as they suckle, I close my eyes as the sensation of them feeding washes over me.

A deep growl startles me and I snap my eyes open to find I'm back in human form. Silas is nowhere to be seen. Raff lays each tiny pup into my arms, scoops us up and carries us into our home. Once inside he takes us into our bedroom and lays me on our bed. He grabs a soft blanket for each of our babies and right before our eyes, each one shifts into the cutest babies I have ever seen.

"We have a girl," I cry and tears stream down my face as I pull her closer to me. Raff lays beside me with our two precious boys in his arms. I watch as he stares into two sets of emerald green eyes with the same flecks that are in his. I turn to gaze into the eyes of our baby girl and notice crystal blue shining back at me.

"You did so well, baby." Raff's voice is deep and husky, he kisses my temple.

"What are we going to name them?"

"I was thinking Jax and Cage for our boys and for our princess, I think your grandmother's name would suit her perfectly."

I nod, loving the names of our boys and knowing it means a lot to my mate to choose them. I gaze down at our little princess and her pink chubby cheeks. "Iris," I whisper and watch as her eyes flutter open and sparkle.

61

I gaze at Raff and nod again, unable to find my voice right now as more tears begin to fall.

After a moment, I peel my eyes away from my daughter and look to my handsome little boys sleeping peacefully in their father's arms. Raff's eyes bounce between our babies and I see how glassy they are before a single tear slides down his cheek.

"You're my forever," I murmur low.

Raff's eyes connect with mine, he wraps his hand behind my neck and pulls me a breath away from his lips.

"One soul. Eternity." He takes my lips in a kiss which speaks the truth of his words.

The End

Next in series:
Book 2
DRAGON'S BLOOD